STAR LIGHT, STAR BRIGHT

MICHAEL KINGSWOOD

CONTENTS

ABOUT THIS BOOK

A plaintive call for help from across the void of space draws the star Alberon's attention, and incites it to compassionate assistance.

But how does a star help something so far away from itself?

Star Light, Star Bright is a 2,100 word scifi short story.

Enjoy the book! After you're done, please come to Michael's website and sign up for his mailing list at www.michaelkingswood.com/newsletter-signup/. Guaranteed to be spam free, he uses it to announce new releases and special promotions for his fans.

STAR LIGHT, STAR BRIGHT

"Star light, star bright
First star I see tonight..."
Alberon shifted its massive bulk as the words came to it, and a small burp of a flare erupted from its southern hemisphere.

The words were not sound; no sound could reach Alberon's consciousness through the Void. But they were plain all the same, carried down one of the infinite photon paths it had sent out over the eons of its existence.

"...I wish I may, I wish I might
Have the wish I wish tonight."
It had heard of supplications such as this, long ago when its siblings first flickered to life in an otherwise cold dust cloud. An older entity, passing near to their nursery on its orbital path, reached out as it sensed their quiescent thoughts and offered guidance, including how to cope with such a plea should they receive one.

But they believed that advice merely jest. Alberon itself certainly never gave it much credence, and indeed by the time the rest of its siblings had drifted too far away to remain easily in contact none had reported ever receiving such a message.

For a few moments, Alberon considered that it may have finally gone mad. That happened to entities without a binary companion unless they take steps to combat it, or so the older one had warned as it passed through. But no, the words definitely were coming from outside of Alberon itself; it was impossible that it made them up.

There was a plaintive nature to the chant that piqued Alberon's curiosity. It had been many revolutions since something new had done that, not since the first sparking of new consciousness on two of Alberon's satellite masses.

If that had happened here, it was logical that consciousness should arise elsewhere on other entities' satellites. But Alberon had never encountered it before.

So it turned its thoughts fully toward the photon pathway that had brought the words.

There was a...warping...in Alberon's perception as it merged its thoughts onto the photon pathway, a compression of time and space until Alberon could sense the entirety of the photon's travel as a single expression.

It had not looked down the pathways for a very long time; the older one had warned against it, and Alberon had long ago learned the wisdom in that advice. The compressed perception limited Alberon painfully, making it lose touch with parts of its body. The last time it had done this, it stayed in a pathway so long that it had unknowingly ejected a coronal mass of such magnitude that it left Alberon weak for a quarter of a revolution until it reached the dust cloud in the shock front of a spiral arm and was able to replenish itself. Only blind geometric luck stopped the ejection from impacting its two inhabited satellites and possibly wiping out the emerging sentients there before they could fully take root.

After that brush with disaster, Alberon had set aside the pathways altogether and contented itself with tending its system, warming and protecting its satellites and watching as the sentients there grew and expanded.

Until now.

Now it looked along the length and breadth of the photon pathway, and immediately found the source of the plea in a small clearing on a hillside on the third satellite of an entity that could have been Alberon's cousin, they were so similar.

The creature was physically very different from the sentients that inhabited the fourth and fifth planets of Alberon's system, but it was clearly in distress. Its garments were torn and dirty, and it seemed to be wounded; fluid flowed from its eyes and down the sides of its head past its mouth. It crouched on the ground, looking up toward its sky with its mouth agape, lips trembling.

A second creature, a bit larger than the first, stood a short distance away, peering through a gap between two large growths of vegetation. A fire a short distance past the stand of vegetation bathed the entire scene in an orange-yellow glow.

"Please bring my Dad and brother back safe," said the smaller creature, and the voice was the same as the one that began the chant which drew Alberon's attention.

A series of loud popping noises in the distance made the larger creature jump slightly. Then it turned, the long loose growths on its head swaying back and forth disconcertingly, and hurried to the smaller's side.

It touched the small one with one of its forelimbs. "They're coming, Heather. We have to go."

The small creature made a snuffing sound, then pushed itself to its feet.

Both paused to sling bags over their forelimbs, and the larger hefted a long, straight cylinder—a weapon of some sort, Alberon supposed. Then they hurried out of the little clearing.

Alberon pondered for a short while, considering. The concept of mother and father, and of siblings, was not foreign to it. The sentients of its two satellites had similar structures, though the two species varied greatly in how they accomplished their procreative activities. What was it that had dragged the other half of the bonding pair away?

Alberon withdrew ever so slightly from the photon path, and the scene it was able to perceive widened, encompassing a land mass that jutted northward from the main continent for a short while before bending west and then south until it pointed at the primary land mass once more. All across the peninsula, groups of sentients were advancing, some afoot and some in metallic vehicles, some in airborne craft. All possessed weapons similar to the one the larger sentient who accompanied Heather—Alberon presumed that was Heather's mother—had carried. The sentients were drawn up in dividing lines, seen from above, and were discharging their weapons into each other. Cities and villages were aflame, and Alberon could see that one group, with features similar to Heather and the other sentient, was retreating in earnest while the other side, obviously a different sub-race, advanced.

At once Alberon understood. It had seen this before.

Long ago, on the fourth satellite in its system, the sentient species had gone to war with itself. The battles raged on through many of the satellite's revolutions, until it appeared that one sub-breed of the species was about to be wiped out.

Thankfully, the sentients on the fifth planet were different. They had started out warring against each other, but very early on one faction emerged triumphant. Unlike the species on the fourth planet, the fifth's winning element proved benevolent, and instead of destroying its rivals, the entire species came together in a single, strong whole. They soon looked out past the borders of their little massive body, and set up on the sub-masses that were satellites of their own home. A short while later, they moved out further and discovered the sentients on Alberon's fourth satellite.

It was the good fortune of the sentients on that mass that the fifth's sentients found them when they did. The fifth's sentients arrived toward the end of what would have been a war of extermination. With their superior ships, weaponry, and numbers, the sentients from the fifth satellite were swiftly able to put an end to the fighting and preserve the lives of the remaining fourth sentients on both sides.

For many hundreds of revolutions after that, Alberon's system remained at peace, with the sentients from the fifth satellite expanding to the remaining bodies in the system, and bringing their cousins from the fourth satellite along with them.

They had since expanded beyond Alberon's system, and though it no longer had contact with those particular entities, from the extensive shipping going back and forth from an ever-increasing number of external systems, Alberon presumed that those colonies were doing well.

It withdrew from the photon pathway linking itself with the alien world and pondered for a time.

The sentient Heather was in need, and more that that, so was its entire species. They clearly were on the verge of eradicating a significant portion of their population. Were that to happen, the consequences for their species could be extreme.

How did their system's entity allow this to happen?

Alberon was not foolish; it knew it was not all-powerful. But it also recalled its own actions when the sentients from its fifth satellite set forth into the Void. It had exerted influence, enough to halt a number of potentially catastrophic problems at least long enough for their early ships to make it back home. And then when they set out to rescue the sentients on the fourth satellite, Alberon had made sure the wavelengths they used for communications were clear, and that their supply ships did not have to endure any untoward troubles during their transit.

That had turned the tide and ensured the fifth's satellite's success.

So why had the entity in Heather's system not...

Alberon's train of thought stopped as the obvious answer sprang into its mind.

The entity could not intervene because in its system sentience only came into existence on one of its satellites, the third.

That entity could not help, but perhaps Alberon could.

It sent its thoughts back down the photon path, evaluating the distance involved.

The sentients from its fifth satellite had journeyed this far before; they could make the trip again.

But how to alert them to the problem?

Alberon drew back up the path again, more slowly this time, and scanned about. Immediately it became clear that the alien world was transmitting a multitude of signals throughout the spectrum. Those signals would be detectable...

But when it removed its thoughts from the photon path, Alberon realized its error. This distance was so great, even it could not detect those transmissions. The fifth satellite sentients surely would not be able to do so either; they already would have, otherwise.

Alberon paused, considering.

When the fifth satellite invaded the fourth, Alberon had maintained the frequencies clear by lensing other emissions around the Void between the planets. A simple trick that required manipulating a certain amount of Alberon's tremendous mass to warp the gravitational paths and magnetic envelope of the system to bend those emissions out of the way.

Perhaps it could generate a similar effect, farther out.

It would mean displacing a large amount of mass. Just the thought of doing that sent a feeling of cold seeping through its core. The loss of fuel would set Alberon back for many hundreds, perhaps thousands, of its satellites' revolutions until it once again reached a spiral arm shock front.

Fortunately, its sentients would probably not notice any large effect. It would simply expand its outer layers to balance out the altered reaction rate in its core and keeps its luminosity more or less constant until it could find more mass.

Doing this was possible.

Alberon could not follow the photon paths that had been emitted by the alien world, only its own. But sending its thoughts down the path it followed before, it was able to locate several transmissions that appeared promising.

It withdrew back to itself again, and paused. This next would require delicate, controlled work.

For a long time, Alberon labored. It would not do to make the change sudden; that would disrupt its own system too much. For several of its satellites' revolutions, it labored until finally, and with less difficulty than it initially thought necessary, the work was done.

The transmissions from the alien world, bent and brightened by the lens, met the sensors of the Fifth satellite's sentients.

Almost immediately, Alberon noticed the transmissions' effect. The chatter on the sentients' frequencies intensified, and over the next several revolutions their masses and sub-masses saw a marked increase in activity: vessels under construction, security force training, new design development, and more.

And then finally, the sentients gathered what they had wrought. An armada of vessels, crewed by thousands of Fifth satellite sentients and their Fourth satellite wards. Most of the vessels bristled with sensor clusters, communication systems, and weapons of every type. Others were mostly unarmed, but carried untold numbers of sentients aboard.

A mighty fleet for a grand mission.

As the vessels departed its system on a trajectory for the third satellite of its cousin, Alberon allowed itself to experience contented pride.

They could not help the sentient Heather. In the time it took the fleet to arrive, the sentient would likely already have terminated. But that would not keep the Fifth satellite sentients from the rest of Heather's species. They would impose order and stop the slaughter, and save these new sentients from themselves.

Just like they had done before on the fourth satellite.

Yes, it was a good thing Alberon had done.

Letting out a little flare in a rare display of prideful joy, Alberon turned its mind to some of its other photon pathways. Perhaps there were still other sentients that needed its help.

MESSAGE FROM THE AUTHOR

Thank you for reading my book. I hope you enjoyed reading it as much as I enjoyed writing it.

Every review helps an author out, so whether you loved this book, hated it, or something in between, please take a minute to tell other readers what you thought. All of the online retailers make it very easy to do, and I would really appreciate it.

Feel free to come say hi at my website or on Facebook. I always enjoy hearing from readers, especially since you all are, collectively, my boss.

I also have a weekly podcast, Story Time With Michael Kingswood, where I read stories and talk through some of the latest goings on in my world. I'd love to see you there.

Thanks again. My best to you and yours.

Warm Regards,
Michael Kingswood

MAILING LIST

If you enjoyed this book and would like word on new releases and special deals from Michael Kingswood, sign up for his newsletter on his website. Guaranteed to be spam-free, you can opt out at any time. And you can rest assured he will not share your information with anyone, for any reason.

https://michaelkingswood.com/newsletter-signup/

SUPPORTING PATRONAGE

Michael would like to invite you to become a supporting member of his website. Similar in concept to Patreon, a few dollars a month will give you access to exclusive content, and help him to focus more of his time to writing fun and exciting stories for your enjoyment.

Sign up at his website:

https://www.michaelkingswood.com/membership/
supporting-patronage/

ABOUT THE AUTHOR

Michael Kingswood is 20-year veteran of the US Navy submarine force and a lifelong fan of science fiction and fantasy literature. His work has appeared in numerous collections and anthologies, to include the Fiction River Anthology series from WMG publishing. He holds a bachelors degree in Mechanical Engineering as well as a Master of Engineering Management and a Master of Business Administration. He has four children and currently resides in San Diego.

Find Michael Kingswood online at:

www.michaelkingswood.com

www.facebook.com/michael.kingswood

steemit.com/@michaelkingswood

MORE BOOKS BY MICHAEL KINGSWOOD

Glimmer Vale Chronicles

Glimmer Vale

Out-Dweller

Tollard's Peak

Robbed Blind

Wedding Gifts: A Glimmer Vale Chronicles Story

The Falconer's Stairs

Glimmer Vale Omnibus Edition #1

The Pericles Conspiracy

Passing In The Night

The Pericles Conspiracy

Dawn Of Enlightenment

Masters Of The Sun

Novellas

What Lurks Between

The Necromancer's Lair

The Champion

Veritas Morte

Story Collections

Tales Of Adventure #1

Tales Of Adventure #2

Short Story 10-Pack

A Jar Of Mixed Treats

Short Fiction

Michael has also published a number of shorter works, links to which can be found on his website.